KATIE KAZOO, SWITCHEROO

Get Lost!

For my swimming buddies,
Marie and Cathy—N.K.

Text copyright © 2003 by Nancy Krulik. Illustrations copyright © 2003 by John and Wendy. All rights reserved. Published by Grosset & Dunlap, a division of Penguin Putnam Books for Young Readers, 345 Hudson Street, New York, NY, 10014. GROSSET & DUNLAP is a trademark of Penguin Putnam Inc. Published simultaneously in Canada. Printed in U.S.A.

Library of Congress Cataloging-in-Publication Data

Krulik, Nancy E.
Get lost! / by Nancy Krulik ; illustrated by John & Wendy.
p. cm.—(Katie Kazoo, switcheroo ; 6)
Summary: Katie Carew's third–grade class spends three days at Science Camp, where Katie magically changes places with the strict Head Counselor while on a hike and gets her group hopelessly lost. Includes directions for making all–natural soap.
[1. Camps—Fiction. 2. Camp counselors—Fiction. 3. Magic—Fiction. 4. Lost children—Fiction.] I. John, ill. II. Wendy, ill. III. Title. IV. Series: Krulik, Nancy E. Katie Kazoo, switcheroo ; 6.
PZ7.K944Ge 2003
[Fic]—dc21

2002015624

ISBN 0-448-43101-7   H I J

Get Lost!

by Nancy Krulik • illustrated by John & Wendy

Grosset & Dunlap

Chapter 1

Katie Carew bent down and kissed her cocker spaniel on the nose. "Don't be afraid, Pepper," she told him. "I'm not going away forever. It's just three days."

Pepper sniffed at Katie's mouth. Then he licked her—right on the lips.

Katie let out a big yawn. It was 7:30 Monday morning. Usually, that was the time Katie got out of bed. But not today. Today Katie had already eaten breakfast. She was already dressed. And she was already at school!

Katie yawned again. She was so tired. She hadn't slept at all the night before. She'd been too nervous. She was about to go away to Science Camp—*for three days and two nights!*

Just then, a big yellow school bus pulled into the parking lot.

"Yahoo! The bus is here!" Manny Gonzalez shouted excitedly. "Science Camp, here we come!"

Katie's class had been talking about Science Camp since the first day of school. The third grade made the trip every year.

Some kids were really excited to go. Katie was more nervous. She had never been away from her family for that long before.

"Hey Katie, are you psyched or what?" Katie's best friend Jeremy Fox called out, as he and his mother walked onto the school playground.

"Or what," Katie answered nervously.

"Come on. Camp is great! I spent two weeks at sleepaway camp last summer. It was the best time of my whole life."

Jeremy was wearing hiking boots and

carrying a water canteen. He'd packed his clothes in a waterproof camp duffel bag. His sleeping bag was made of camouflage material.

Katie was wearing her everyday sneakers. Her mother had packed her clothes in the beat-up suitcase she used when she visited her grandma. Suddenly, Katie's Cuddle Bears sleeping bag seemed kind of babyish.

Katie's mom gave her a big squeeze. "You're going to have a great time. It's only two nights. Think of it as a long sleepover." Mrs. Carew pointed toward the edge of the playground. "Oh, look—here comes Suzanne!"

Suzanne Lock was Katie's other best friend. Katie figured she must have been planning for a *really* long sleepover. After all, she was wheeling a *huge* hot pink suitcase and carrying a small overnight bag. Her father was carrying the matching duffel bag.

Quickly, Katie hurried over to help Suzanne with her bags.

"Why do you have so much stuff?" Katie asked as she took the overnight bag from her friend. It was very heavy.

"A girl's got to be prepared for anything, Katie." Suzanne smiled as she unloaded the rest of her luggage beside Katie's. "If it's cold at night, I'll need a jacket. If it's warm during the day, I'll need shorts. And I don't want to wear the same outfit at night that I wore all day, so . . . "

"We're going *camping!*" Jeremy shouted. "You're supposed to rough it!"

"I am! I didn't bring my blow-dryer."

Katie giggled. She was scared to go to Science Camp, but she was glad her two best friends would be there with her. She loved them both—even if they didn't always like each other.

"Hey, Katie, have you seen George?" Kevin Camilleri asked as he came running over. "Manny and I have to talk to him."

"I don't think he's here yet," Katie told him. "What's so important?"

"It's a secret," Kevin said. "We aren't telling anyone but George."

Just then, Mrs. Derkman stepped onto the playground. Katie could hardly believe that this was her teacher. Usually, Mrs. Derkman wore dresses and high heels. Her hair was always perfect, and she smelled like sweet perfume.

But today, Mrs. Derkman was a mess! She was wearing sweatpants and sneakers. Her hair was covered by a huge, floppy hat. Worst of all, she smelled like bug spray.

"Whoa! Check out Mrs. Derkman!" Kevin shouted. "She looks like a regular person."

A tall man with a beard and moustache walked over to Mrs. Derkman. "Here are your bags, honey," he said. "Your suitcase is so heavy. What do you have in there?"

"Bug spray, bug candles, and bug cream," Mrs. Derkman answered. "Those creatures aren't getting anywhere near me this year!"

"Did you hear him?" Kevin whispered to Katie. "He called Mrs. Derkman *honey*."

"That must be Mr. Derkman," Katie's mom said to Mrs. Fox. "He seems very nice."

Katie gasped. *Mrs. Derkman's husband?*

"We'd better go now," Mrs. Derkman said,

nervously looking at her watch.

Mr. Derkman smiled. "See you in three days," he said. "Don't let the bedbugs bite!"

Mrs. Derkman's eyes bulged. "Don't say that!" she squawked. Then she kissed her husband on the cheek.

The kids stared at their teacher in amazement.

"Okay, class, let's get on the bus!" Mrs. Derkman ordered her class. "We have no time to waste."

Katie sighed. Mrs. Derkman still *sounded* like herself.

"Well, this is it, sweetie," said Katie's mom. "Better get on line."

"You'll stay until the bus leaves?" Katie asked nervously.

Her mom nodded. "Of course, honey."

Katie gave Pepper one last pat, and then headed toward the bus. But before she could get on board, Manny started to yell.

"Mrs. Derkman, we can't leave!" He shouted out. "George isn't here yet!"

The kids all looked around. Where could George Brennan be?

Chapter 2

"Please, Mrs. Derkman, we have to wait!" Manny begged as the class began to board the bus. "Camp won't be fun without George!"

"We still have a few minutes before all the luggage is loaded onto the bus," Mrs. Derkman assured him. "I'm sure George will be here by then."

Katie found a seat near the window in the middle of the bus. Suzanne hopped into the seat beside her.

"Do you think George is coming?" Katie asked Suzanne as the girls buckled their seat belts.

"I won't miss him if he doesn't. George is

always telling dumb jokes," Suzanne said.

Katie frowned. Sometimes Suzanne could be pretty mean. Katie liked George's jokes. They were really funny. She liked George, too. He was the one who had given Katie her extremely cool nickname—Katie Kazoo.

"I hope we don't have to wait around all day for him," Jeremy said, as he took the seat across the aisle from Katie and Suzanne. "I want to get to camp!"

"There he is!" Kevin's voice rang out from the back of the bus. "Hurry up, George!" he shouted through the open window.

But George wasn't hurrying. In fact, it looked as though his dad was dragging him across the playground to the bus. George had a very angry scowl on his face.

Mr. Brennan marched George straight up to the yellow bus. "Have a good time, son," Mr. Brennan said.

"Fat chance," George barked back.

Mr. Brennan sighed. "It's just a few days at

Science Camp, George. It's not like you're joining the army."

George didn't answer. He walked to the back of the bus and plopped down in the seat across from Manny and Kevin.

Kevin smiled at his pal. "Am I glad to see you. You wouldn't believe the amazing things I snuck into my suitcase." Kevin leaned over to whisper in George's ear. "I packed all kinds of practical joke stuff—plastic bugs, pepper gum, and a whoopee cushion."

Usually, George was really into things like whoopee cushions. But not today. He just sat there, staring out the window with his hands crossed over his chest. "Big deal," he muttered.

Kevin looked surprised. "Come on. We're going to have so much fun!"

George shook his head. "No we're not. This whole Science Camp thing is dumb."

Jeremy looked back at him. "You're nuts, George. Camp's the best. "I should know.

I went to camp last summer."

Suzanne sighed. "You've only told us that about a million times."

"Well, I don't think camp's cool," George argued. "Who wants to go to camp when you can sleep in your own bed and have cable TV?"

As the bus drove away, Katie looked out the window and watched her mother become smaller and smaller. Soon, Katie couldn't see her mom at all. A really lonely feeling came over her.

Katie wasn't the only one feeling sad. Katie could see a tear falling down the side of Suzanne's face.

"Hey, you want to share a bunk bed?" Katie asked, trying to cheer her pal.

Suzanne smiled . . . a little. "Can I have the top?"

"Sure."

Jeremy turned to Katie and Suzanne. "You guys want to hear a camp cheer?" he asked.

"Why not?" Suzanne said.

Jeremy smiled broadly as he began to cheer.
"Brrr. It's cold in here. There must be 3A in
the atmosphere. All hands clap. All feet stamp.
We're the coolest kids at Science Camp!"

Soon the kids in class 3A were shouting Jeremy's cheer. Mandy Banks and Miriam Chan were even doing a hand-clapping game to the rhythm. Everyone was having fun.

Everyone except George. He looked miserable.

Katie joined in. She felt a little bit better. As Katie looked over at Jeremy's smiling face, she hoped that she would be as happy at camp as he'd been.

But Katie couldn't help feeling that something awful was going to happen at Science Camp.

Chapter 3

As the bus turned a corner, the kids caught a glimpse of the camp sign. Suddenly, everyone seemed to be talking at once.

Everyone but George, that is. He sat there like a lump.

"We're here, because we're here, because we're here, because we're here . . . " Jeremy began singing another one of his camp songs.

"Ooh, are those the cabins?" Mandy asked, pointing to the tiny little wooden huts that dotted the campgrounds.

"Did you see that lake?" Zoe added. "It's so blue."

"I wonder where the nature shack is,"

Manny said. "Mrs. Derkman told me they have goats and sheep there."

"Do you think they have full-length mirrors in the cabins?" Suzanne asked.

Before Katie could answer, the bus rolled to a stop. Immediately, the kids unbuckled their belts and bolted for the door.

One by one the children filed off the bus. Katie looked around. Science Camp was really pretty. The trees were blossoming. She could hear birds singing in the distance. And there was a clean smell to the breeze that circled gently around her head.

The breeze!

Suddenly Katie had a nervous feeling in the pit of her stomach.

Quickly she looked at her classmates. Their hair was blowing in the wind, too.

She stared at the trees. The leaves and blossoms were moving. *Phew*. It was just a normal, everyday breeze. For a moment there, Katie had been afraid that the *magic wind*

had followed her all the way to Science Camp.

The magic wind was a tornado-like wind that twisted and turned—but only around Katie. It was really scary. But the scariest part happened after the wind *stopped* blowing. That's when Katie turned into someone else!

It all started one really awful day. Katie had ruined her favorite jeans and burped in front of the whole class. That had been so embarrassing. Katie had wished that she could be anyone but herself.

There must have been a shooting star flying overhead or something when she made that wish, because the very next day, the magic wind blew, turning Katie into Speedy, the class hamster! Katie had spent a whole morning gnawing on wooden chew sticks and running on a hamster wheel.

Luckily, Katie had changed back into herself before anyone stepped on her!

Katie never knew who the magic wind might turn her into next. Already it had switcherooed her into the school lunch lady, Lucille, and the principal, Mr. Kane. And once the magic wind turned Katie into *Jeremy*. What a mess that had been!

Katie never knew when the magic wind was coming. She just hoped that the wind wouldn't be able to find her at Science Camp. It was going to be hard enough being away from home. She didn't want to have to be away from her body, too.

Chapter 4

Manny, George, and Kevin were all huddled together on the grass behind the bus. Manny and Kevin were whispering to each other and giggling. George just looked bored.

Finally, Manny walked up to Mrs. Derkman and stared at her arm. At first, he didn't say anything. Then he asked her, "Mrs. Derkman, what's black and green, has six legs, a furry body, and two antennae?"

Mrs. Derkman shrugged. "I don't know, Manny."

"I don't know either, but it's crawling up your arm!" Manny told her.

"*Aaaahhhhhh!*" Mrs. Derkman screamed

so loud, Katie was sure they could hear her back at Cherrydale Elementary School. The teacher jumped up and down, slapping her arm. "Get it off me! Get it off me right now!"

Suddenly, a woman with a deep, booming voice came up behind Mrs. Derkman. "What is going on here?" she demanded.

Katie gasped. The woman was very tall. Her muscles were bulging out of her green army uniform. She looked like she never smiled . . . ever. She seemed scarier than any bug.

"Th-th-there's a hairy bug on my arm," Mrs. Derkman stammered.

"Oh, give me a break," the woman in the army uniform barked. "Bugs are part of life out here. Get used to it, soldier."

Soldier?

Mrs. Derkman looked at her curiously. "Excuse me?" she asked.

"Um . . . I mean, there's nothing on your arm," the woman said.

Mrs. Derkman glanced at her bugless arm and sighed. "George Brennan, come here!"

George moped his way over toward the teacher. "I didn't do anything," he insisted.

"Maybe not. But I have a feeling that was your idea of a joke," Mrs. Derkman said.

"It wasn't. Honest," George insisted.

"I wouldn't worry about any more jokes." The woman in the uniform assured Mrs. Derkman. "I'm Genie Manzini, the head counselor. I don't allow for any joking at Science Camp." Genie glared at George.

"Maybe we should call her Genie the *Meanie,*" Suzanne whispered to Katie.

Katie wanted to laugh, but she didn't dare. Who knew what Genie the Meanie might do?

"Okay troops . . . I mean, *boys and girls,*" Genie corrected herself. "I want you to meet the staff. To begin with, I am the head coun-selor. *Everyone* here answers to me."

The children all turned around to see what Mrs. Derkman would say to that. Mrs. Derkman didn't like answering to anyone.

But Mrs. Derkman didn't seem to have heard anything Genie had said. She was too busy spraying herself with bug spray. "Get off me, you miserable ant!" The teacher muttered as she sprayed her sneaker.

Genie pointed to a small woman with short brown hair and a cheery smile. "This is Tess," she said. "She runs our animal program."

"Hi everyone," Tess greeted them. "I hope you will all visit the nature shack and help with the animals."

Katie grinned. Tess seemed nice. And maybe visiting the animals in the nature shack would keep her from missing Pepper so much.

"And this is Carson, our nature arts instructor," Genie said, pointing to a tall, thin man wearing sunglasses and a tie-dyed T-shirt.

"You won't believe all the things we can create with nature's art supplies," Carson told them. "We're going to have fun here, right?"

"Right!" the kids shouted back.

Genie did not look pleased.

Just then, a loud bell rang out over the campground. "Okay, that means chow time,"

Genie told them. "You have exactly twenty-seven minutes for lunch. Now line up."

The kids formed a straight line.

"March," Genie ordered. "Hup, two, three, four. Hup, two, three . . . "

As Katie marched toward the mess hall, she remembered what George's father had said about Science Camp not being the army.

Mr. Brennan couldn't have been more wrong.

Chapter 5

Genie the Meanie kept the kids moving all day long. They went from morning to night without a rest. Some of the activities—like making beeswax candles and feeding the animals—were kind of fun.

But Genie never once let the kids forget that Science Camp was part of school. She made them carry notebooks and pencils everywhere, so they could take notes on what they learned.

"I'm exhausted," Katie said as she flopped down on the bottom bunk.

"All I know is Science Camp made me really tired," Miriam added. "I think I could fall asleep anywhere. Even on this lumpy bed."

Suzanne put her foot on the metal edge of Katie's bed and hopped up onto her top bunk.

The top bunk sagged slightly over Katie's head. The sagging lump moved back and forth as Suzanne found a comfortable spot to lie down. For a minute, Katie thought the bed might come down on top of her.

It was easier not to look up, so instead Katie looked around the cabin. There were four bunk beds lined up along the walls. The walls of the cabin were made of pine-colored wood paneling. There were four screened-in windows on each wall.

Just then, the cabin door swung open. "Okay, girls, it's time for lights out," Tess said, as she walked in and flicked off the light.

As Tess left the cabin, Katie felt scared . . . and lonely. Pepper always slept on her bed with her at home. Now she was all alone.

Suddenly, Katie heard leaves rustling outside the bunk. "Suzanne," she whispered.

"Do you hear that?"

Suzanne listened for a second. "I think there's someone out there."

"Someone or some*thing*," Miriam suggested nervously.

Zoe leaped out of her bed and ran over to

where Katie was sleeping. "Do you mind if I just sit here?" she asked Katie. "I don't think I want to be so close to the door."

The crunching of the leaves was louder now. Whatever was out there was getting closer.

"Do you think it's a bear?" Katie asked.

"Maybe it's a monster," Mandy suggested. "A monster who hates kids at Science Camp."

Suddenly, a huge light beam came shining in through the cabin window.

"*Aaaaaaaaaahhhhhhhhh!*" The girls all screamed. "It's the Science Camp monster!"

But the light wasn't coming from a monster. It was coming from Genie the Meanie's flashlight.

"All right, boys, I see you out there," Genie shouted. "You've been bunkhopping!"

The girls all raced to the windows to see what was happening. In the glare of Genie's light, they could see Kevin and Manny's faces.

"I've got the perfect punishment for you two," Genie assured them in a voice that made the boys shake.

The head counselor grabbed Manny by the hand and walked him over to a huge old pine tree. "Hug it!" Genie ordered.

"Hug what?" Manny asked.

"The tree. *Hug the tree,*" Genie ordered again. She turned to Kevin. "You hug the one next to it. That way I can be sure you boys aren't going anywhere."

Kevin had no choice. He reached out his arms and hugged the tree. Manny did the same.

The girls knew they were supposed to be quiet after lights out. But they couldn't help it. The sight of Manny and Kevin hugging trees was just too funny. They all started to laugh.

And Genie the Meanie didn't tell them to stop.

Chapter 6

"What's that sticky stuff in your hair?" Carson asked Kevin, as everyone entered the mess hall for breakfast the next morning.

"Pine sap," Kevin replied.

"How'd you get that on your head?" the nature arts counselor asked.

Kevin moaned and tried to wipe his hair. "I don't want to talk about it."

Kevin took his tray and sat down beside Katie, Jeremy, Suzanne, and Manny.

"What's up with George?" Suzanne asked Kevin. "I thought you guys always sat together."

It was true. George, Manny, and Kevin

usually did everything together.

But today, George was sitting all by himself in the back of the mess hall. He looked miserable.

"I don't know what his problem is," Manny said. "He doesn't want to do anything. Like last night. We were all telling ghost stories in the cabin. George went to sleep!"'

"That doesn't sound like George," Katie agreed. "He loves scary stuff."

"So, Jeremy, when exactly is this place going to get fun?" Suzanne asked, changing the subject. "You keep talking about how great camp is, but I think Science Camp is a real drag."

Jeremy nodded. "This isn't like the camp I went to last summer," he agreed. "But maybe today we'll get to to play some games or something."

Just then, Genie passed by the table. Jeremy smiled nervously in her direction. "Excuse me, Genie."

The head counselor glared down at him. "What is it soldier . . . I mean *student?*"

"Are we going to have some free time today?" Jeremy asked. "Maybe we can play soccer or basketball or something. You know, have a little fun."

Genie's eyes opened wide. "This is not summer camp!" she shouted. "This is Science Camp. You are not here to play. You are here to learn. And nobody said learning has to be fun!"

Jeremy gulped. Genie sure sounded mad.

"I have a full schedule for you kids," she continued. "It begins with inspection. I'm going to check each of your cabins for neatness. And your beds had better be made well. I want those sheets pulled so tight I can bounce a quarter off them!"

"What does bouncing quarters on beds have to do with science?" Manny wondered aloud, after Genie walked away.

As the kids chowed down on their eggs,

Katie glanced over at George. He seemed very quiet. She was worried about him. Finally, she got up and walked over to sit beside her friend.

"Hey, George," Katie greeted him.

George didn't say anything. He just shoved a forkful of eggs into his mouth. "These are gross," he muttered between bites.

"I know egg-zactly what you mean," Katie joked.

George didn't laugh. Instead, he took another forkful of eggs.

"Are you looking forward to our hike this afternoon?" Katie asked, changing the subject.

George rolled his eyes. "No," he snapped. "Hikes are dumb. Everything here is dumb."

"George, why are you being so mean?"

"I'm not being mean. I'm just too cool for this place," George told her. "Can I help it if you're not?"

Katie's face got red. "That was a mean

thing to say, George Brennan!" she shouted. "I don't think you're cool at all. I think you're a jerk!"

Then, Katie got up and stormed out of the mess hall—before Mrs. Derkman had a chance to tell her that *jerk* isn't a word you use in school.

Chapter 7

After Genie had inspected their cabins, the kids in 3A gathered on the main lawn to get ready for their hikes. They each had their own water bottles and a bag of cookout food to carry.

Cookie, the camp cook, smiled at Katie as she handed her a bag. "There's no meat in yours," she assured Katie. Cookie knew that Katie was a vegetarian. "But I added extra carrot sticks and potato chips. I don't let kids go hungry."

"Thanks," Katie said with a grin.

The class had been split into small groups for their hikes. Katie, Suzanne, Jeremy and

George were in the same group.

"Who's our leader, anyway?" George asked. "Mrs. Derkman," Suzanne said.

Katie frowned. " I was hoping Tess or Carson could be our leader."

Just then Genie walked toward Katie and her friends. "Mrs. Derkman has a bad case of poison ivy," she told them. "She fell in a patch of it while running away from an oncoming fly. I'll be taking you on your hike.

"Okay, troops. March," Genie ordered. "Left, right, left, right."

Katie got in line behind George. He was going very slowly. "You'd better march faster," Katie told him. "Genie the Meanie is going to yell at you."

George reached into his pocket and pulled out a hard candy wrapped in shiny paper. "What's the hurry?" he mumbled as he sucked on the candy. "It's not like we're going any- where. It's a hike to nowhere."

"We're supposed to be looking at the

plants and animals in the woods," Katie reminded him. "See, there's a chipmunk." George was not impressed.

After they'd been hiking for a while, Katie marched up to the front of the line. "Genie," she asked quietly. "Are we anywhere near a bathroom?"

Genie pointed out into the woods.

"Behind that tree. Or that tree. Or any tree," Genie told her.

Katie gulped. "You mean I have to pee in the woods?"

Genie nodded. "Or hold it in."

That settled it. Katie ran off in the direction of a huge oak tree surrounded by some high shrubs. She hoped the bushes would hide her.

Suddenly, Katie felt a cold breeze on the back of her neck. The light wind felt great after the long hike she'd been on . . .until Katie realized that the wind wasn't blowing anywhere but on her.

This was no ordinary wind. This was the magic wind!

Oh no, Katie thought. *Not here. Not in the middle of the woods!*

The magic wind began spinning faster and faster, all around Katie. She shut her eyes tightly, and tried not to cry. As the fierce tornado swirled, she held on to the tree. She struggled to keep her feet on the ground. The wind just kept getting more and more powerful.

And then it stopped.

Katie was afraid to open her eyes. What if the wind had blown her away. What if she was all alone in the middle of the forest?

But Katie was *not* alone. The other kids were right nearby.

As Katie opened her eyes, Jeremy stared up at her.

"Genie?" he asked. "Why are you hugging that tree?"

Chapter 8

Katie looked down at her feet. Instead of her own bright red sneakers, she saw Genie's hiking boots. And she was wearing army pants instead of jeans.

Katie had become Genie the Meanie!

Uh-oh. Genie was in charge of the hike. She was supposed to teach the kids to build a fire, cook the food, and find the way back to camp.

Katie didn't know how to do any of those things.

"Hey, what happened to Katie?" George asked. "She's been gone a long time."

Katie gulped. She knew exactly where Katie was. But how could she explain that to her friends?

"Katie!" Jeremy called into the woods.

There was no answer.

"Katie Kazoo, quit goofing around," George shouted.

Suzanne began to panic. "She's missing!"

"Relax, she didn't go far," Katie assured her. "I'm sure if we just sit here she'll come back."

Suzanne was so scared she forgot to be afraid of Genie the Meanie. "We can't just sit here!" she declared. "She's lost in the woods somewhere. We've got to look for her!"

Katie didn't know what to do do. The real Genie probably would have searched for her. That was her job—to keep everyone safe.

"All right. We'll look for your friend. But let's be sure to stick together. I don't want to lose any more of you," Katie said, trying to sound like the real Genie the Meanie.

As the kids wandered through the woods, searching for their missing friend, Katie tried her best to act like a real head counselor. It wasn't easy. Katie had never been out in the woods before.

The kids were starting to panic. Katie had to do something to calm them down. She decided to change the subject. That's what a real head counselor would do—get the kids thinking about something else.

Katie pointed to a patch of leaves on the ground. Each of the green leaves had three parts. "Look at that beautiful plant," Katie said. She bent down to pick up a leaf.

"Genie, don't touch that!" Jeremy shouted. "That's poison ivy."

Oops! Katie gulped. What a mistake that would have been.

"Very good, Jeremy," Katie said. "I *meant* to do that. It was a test. I wanted to see if you kids could recognize poison ivy."

"I don't want to look at leaves," Suzanne

moaned. "I want to look for Katie."

"Or what's left of Katie," George added.

"Cut that out, George!" Suzanne shouted.

"Make me!" George screamed back.

Katie leaped between them. "Let's just keep walking," she ordered.

"Which way?" George groaned.

Katie led the kids down a dirt path. "Maybe she headed east," Katie told the kids. "We'll try that way."

"Uh, Genie," Jeremy interrupted, as Katie turned to her right. "We're actually heading west."

"How do you know?" Katie asked him.

"It's almost sunset. The sun sets in the west. It's in front of us right now."

Katie sighed. She didn't know any of this stuff. "Of course," Katie said. "I meant west. We'll head west."

"It's getting kind of dark," Suzanne moaned, as the kids walked behind Katie.

"That's just a cloud over the sun," Katie

assured her, trying to sound confident.

"Actually, I think it's getting dark because it's about six o'clock," Jeremy told her. "It'll be night soon."

"Oh, no!" Suzanne shouted. "Katie will be all alone in the woods at night!"

"Relax, Suzanne," Katie said. "We'll find your friend."

"Katie's not just any friend," Suzanne said. "She's my best friend. I'm worried about her." She looked at George and Jeremy. "Which is more than I can say for some people."

"Hey, she's my best friend, too," Jeremy argued.

"But you don't sound very worried," Suzanne told him.

"I am too worried," Jeremy said.

Katie sighed. "Please stop . . .Whoa!" Before Katie could finish her sentence, she went sliding down a long, slippery slope. When she reached the bottom, she found herself waist deep in thick, gooey mud!

"*Help!* Quicksand!" Katie shouted out. She looked up at George, Jeremy, and Suzanne. "I'm sinking! Help me!"

George stared down at the head counselor. "I'm not helping her," he told Jeremy and Suzanne. "Let the quicksand swallow her up."

"But she's the only one who knows the way back to camp!" Suzanne declared. "And now she's sinking into quicksand!"

"She's not sinking," Jeremy assured her. "And that's not quicksand. It's just a mudslide. We played on one of those at my summer camp. Genie, just grab on to that tree branch and pull yourself back up the hill." Katie did as she was told. She grabbed on to a low-lying branch and tried to pull herself up. It wasn't easy. The mud had made her hands slippery, and the hill was steep.

"Whoa!" Katie cried out, as she slipped back down the mudslide. She fell backward, tripped over a rock, and went rolling into the woods.

Finally, she landed in a thick pile of leaves. Frantically, Katie tried to find a path back up the hill. But there was mud everywhere. Every time she tried to move up the hill, she'd slide back down.

And then, suddenly, she felt a familiar breeze hit the back of her neck.

The magic wind was back!

Wild tornado-like gusts swirled all around Katie's body. She grasped at a nearby tree, but it was out of her reach.

Bam! The strong wind knocked Katie off her feet. She fell to the ground with a *thud*. The wind was the fiercest it had ever been. Katie grabbed on to a huge rock. Her feet flew up in the air, but she refused to let go of that rock. She held on tightly.

And then the wind stopped.

Everything around her was perfectly calm.

Everything except Genie the Meanie, that is. She was lying on the ground, clutching a rock. And she wasn't at all

sure how she'd gotten there.

Genie looked down at her clothes. Her army pants were covered with mud. "What happened? What's going on here?" Genie barked to Katie, who was now standing beside her.

Katie knew she had to say something. "I'm so glad you found me," she blurted out. "I've been lost so long. You're a great counselor, Genie."

"*Head* counselor," Genie reminded her. She scrambled to her feet. Then she looked at Katie curiously. "You were lost?" she asked.

Katie grinned. "Of course. How else could you have found me?"

Chapter 9

"Okay, soldier, just another few feet,"
Genie shouted back to Katie. "Try to climb at
the same time I do." Genie had wrapped her
belt around Katie's waist. She was using the
belt to tow Katie up the slippery hill.

Katie planted her feet firmly into the mud
and tried to climb. "This is hard," she
moaned.

"Almost there," Genie assured her.

"Hey, look," George cried out. "It's Katie
Kazoo!"

As Katie and Genie wandered back toward
the others, Jeremy raced over to them. "Where
were you?" he demanded.

"I went into the woods to . . .to . . ."

"She went to pee." George giggled.

Katie blushed. "Anyway, I got lost, and Genie found me."

"Just in time," George said. "I'm starving. We never got to have our cookout because we were looking for you. Let's just get back to camp and eat something."

"Which way do we go?" Jeremy asked.

Genie's eyes confidently scanned the trees. Suddenly, her face fell. "Where are the red ribbons?" she muttered.

"What ribbons?" Katie asked.

"The red ribbons!" Genie exclaimed, sounding very nervous. "The ones that are tied to the trees. They mark the path back to camp."

"We must have wandered off the path when we were looking for Katie," Jeremy thought aloud. "Can't we take another path?"

"We could," Genie agreed, "if I knew one. But I have no idea how far we are from camp or which way to turn to go back. I'm not even sure how we got here. It's all sort of a blur."

"This is all your fault, Katie Kazoo," George snapped.

Katie stared at George. Did he know that it was she, not Genie, who had gotten them lost? Did George know about magic wind?

"If you hadn't disappeared, we wouldn't have had to look for you," George continued.

Okay, so George didn't know about the magic wind. But he was right. She was the reason the kids were lost. And now even Genie couldn't get them back safely.

"I hate the dark. I hate it," Suzanne blubbered. "We don't even have a flashlight."

"What if there really is a Science Camp monster out there? He could get us." George's eyes grew big. His lip quivered, but he didn't cry. He just stared out into the woods.

Even Jeremy seemed nervous. "Do you think the other kids in our class are worried about us?" he asked.

"Maybe they'll call the police to come look for us," Suzanne said.

"I'll bet Mrs. Derkman is a total wreck," George added. "You know how she can get."

"I doubt it," Katie said. "I'll bet she's fine. She knows we're with the head counselor. Genie can take care of us."

Hoot!

"What was that?" Genie cried out.

Katie gulped. Maybe Genie wouldn't be able to take care of them after all. It seemed that even the head counselor was scared to be in the woods at night.

"I think it was an owl," Katie told her. "Tess said there were a lot of owls in these woods. Don't worry, owls won't hurt you."

Grrrr. Just then, everyone heard a loud grumbling noise.

"Now what was *that?*" Genie wailed.

Katie giggled. "George's stomach."

"It always makes that noise when I'm hungry," George moaned.

"Well, we still have all our cookout supplies," Jeremy suggested. "We could eat. All we have to do is build a fire."

"I don't know how," Suzanne said. "My dad always does the grilling at our house."

The kids looked to Genie for help, but the head counselor was busy staring into the woods. "Where are those ribbons?" she kept saying over and over. "I need my ribbons."

"We're going to have to do this ourselves," Katie told her friends. She was trying to act like a head counselor. After all, she'd been Genie—for a little while, anyway. "Jeremy, did they teach you to make a fire at your camp?"

Jeremy nodded. "I can build one. But we're not allowed to use matches, remember?"

"Genie can handle that," Katie said. "You just tell us how to do the rest."

Jeremy pointed to some fallen branches nearby. "Suzanne, you and Katie go collect sticks. Start with little twigs, and then get bigger ones. Make sure the wood is dry.

George, you and I will get some wood, too."

Before long, the kids had plenty of wood. Jeremy showed them how to build a little box of twigs. Genie lit the twigs with her matches. Then she and Jeremy built up the fire, by throwing logs onto the flames.

There was plenty of food to cook. Jeremy, Suzanne, and George cooked hot dogs on

sticks. Katie ate carrot sticks and potato chips. Then the kids toasted marshmallows.

Genie didn't eat anything. She just sat by the fire, staring into the woods.

When the kids were finished with their food, Katie turned to Genie. "We should put the fire out, right?" she asked.

Genie nodded. She seemed to have finally calmed down. At least she wasn't mumbling about the red ribbons anymore. "We shouldn't leave it burning while we sleep," she told Katie.

"Sleep?" Suzanne asked. "Sleep where?"

Genie emptied her canteen of water on the fire. Katie and Jeremy did the same. "We're going to have to sleep here tonight," Genie told the kids, as the last of the flames disappeared. It was dark now. The moon was the only light they had.

"Sleep on the hard ground?" Suzanne asked. "With all that dirt?"

"What's the matter?" Jeremy asked her.

"You didn't bring the right clothes for sleeping outside?"

Suzanne made a face, but didn't say anything.

Katie grabbed a paper garbage bag and began filling it with soft leaves.

"What are you doing?" Suzanne asked her.

"Making a pillow," she answered.

That seemed like a good idea. The kids all grabbed bags and began to make their own pillows. Katie made an extra one for Genie. She felt bad for her. None of this had really been her fault.

Katie yawned. Her eyes were feeling heavy. She lay down and put her head on her pillow. Before she knew what was happening, Katie was asleep.

Chapter 10

Katie hadn't been asleep very long when she heard footsteps in the woods. There was someone prowling around the campsite!

Katie looked at Genie. She was curled up in a ball, snoring away. She wasn't going to be any help.

Now a quiet sniffling noise was coming from where the fire had been.

Slowly, Katie stood and walked in the direction of the sniffles.

There was George. He was wide awake— and he'd been crying.

"George, what's wrong?" she asked him.

George wiped his nose with his sleeve.

"Nothing," he mumbled.

"Come on, George," Katie urged. "I know something's wrong."

"You're gonna laugh" he said quietly.

"No, I won't. I promise."

"I'm scared," George whispered. "I've never been away from home before."

Katie understood that feeling perfectly. Now she knew why George had acted so

grumpy. He didn't want anyone to know.

"You won't tell, will you?" he begged.

"Never." Katie looked around. Everyone else was sleeping. "I have a great idea. Let's stay up all night and see the sun rise.

George smiled a little. "We can tell jokes and stories and stuff."

"Okay," Katie agreed. "Want to see a neat trick?" She put on the hood of her sweatshirt. Then she pulled the strings really tight so the hood closed around her face.

"That's funny," George said. "You look like a faceless monster."

"A faceless Science Camp monster," Katie giggled.

"Do you know what fairy tale gives a monster the shivers?" George asked her.

Katie shook her head.

"Ghoul-dilocks and the Three Brrrrs!" he laughed at his own joke.

Katie grinned. George was back to normal. One problem solved.

Chapter 11

The next morning, the group was up early. They wanted to get back to camp right away.

"Can you find the right path now?" Jeremy asked Genie hopefully.

"I'm not sure," she replied.

Katie could tell that her friends were getting scared again. But somehow, things seemed less frightening in the sunlight.

"I'm hungry," George moaned. "Do we have any food left from last night? Maybe a hot dog or something?"

Suzanne made a face. "Hot dogs for breakfast? Yuck!"

"I'll eat anything when I'm this starved," George told her.

Katie checked the food pack. It was empty. "We don't have any food left,"

George looked upset. Then, suddenly, he brightened. "Yes, we do," he said. "I have those candies I brought on the hike."

At first Genie seemed angry. "You brought candy on the hike?" Then her stomach growled. "I'll take one," she added.

George reached into his pocket. Then he frowned as he pulled out an empty hand. "This is terrible!"

"What?" Katie asked. "Did you finish them all?"

George shook his head. "There's a hole in my pocket. The candies fell out."

"Oh, no!" Jeremy moaned. "That's awful."

Just then, Katie spotted a shiny round object over by a tree. A few feet away she saw another one . . . and then another. Katie raced over and picked up one of the shiny things.

"It's not awful at all," she told the others.

"George just saved us!"

"How did I do that?" he asked her.

"These are your candies," Katie told him, holding up a shiny wrapped treat. "They must have been falling out of your pocket the whole time we were hiking. All we have to do is follow the trail of candies. They'll lead us back to camp. And we can eat as we hike," she added, popping a butterscotch into her mouth.

Chapter 12

The tired hikers arrived back at camp before their friends woke up. In fact, the whole camp was still asleep—except for Cookie. She was waiting for them outside the Mess Hall.

"Where have you all been?" she asked, as Genie and the kids walked onto the camp-grounds. "I was up all night worrying. If you didn't come back soon, I was going to have send out a search party."

"It's a long story," Genie told Cookie.

"We got lost. We slept in the woods. And now we're back," Jeremy explained.

"Well, it's sure good to see you," Cookie told them. "Why don't you all take showers? Then

I'll make you a special treat for breakfast.
You look starved."

That sounded great to Katie. She was really
hungry.

"There's something else I have to do first,"
George said, as he ran off in the direction of
the cabins.

"You know, that was actually kind of fun,"
Jeremy told Katie and Suzanne as they
walked.

"Wait until the other kids hear what a
wimp Genie turned out to be!" Suzanne
laughed.

Katie shook her head. "I don't think we
should tell the other kids about that. It's not
nice to make fun of her for being scared."

"But she acted so tough before . . ."
Suzanne began.

"She was just doing her job," Katie told
her. "She had to be tough. It's a lot of respon-
sibility being a head counselor. You're in
charge of everything."

Before Suzanne could argue, the kids heard a loud scream coming from one of the cabins.

"*Spider. . . on my pillow!*"

Mrs. Derkman came racing out of her cabin. Her face was dotted with big blobs of pink lotion. Her hair was wrapped up in curlers. She was wearing a polka-dot flannel nightgown and a pair of fuzzy yellow slippers. She looked awful.

"Wow, check out Mrs. Derkman!" Suzanne exclaimed.

"Oh, no!" Katie gasped.

Jeremy couldn't say anything. He was laughing too hard.

As Mrs. Derkman stood in the middle of the campground screaming, George snuck out of her cabin with a big smile on his face. He ran off before the teacher could spot him.

Katie glanced at Genie. She was looking right in the direction of Mrs. Derkman's cabin. There was no way she could have missed seeing George run out of there.

Katie frowned. Was Genie going to punish George?

But Genie didn't yell or even call George over. Instead, she walked over to Katie and her friends, and laughed along with them.

Chapter 13

Katie was really sad when the time came to get on the bus and drive back to Cherrydale. Science Camp had been really fun. She was going to miss the bunnies in the nature shack and Cookie's chocolate-chip cookies.

But mostly Katie was going to miss Genie.

It turned out that the head counselor could be really nice when she wanted to. She taught the kids how to melt chocolate and marshmallows on graham crackers to make s'mores. And she showed them how to make beads out of clay that they dug from the ground.

WELCOME TO

PINE ↟ HILL

"Maybe we can come back here again in fourth grade," Katie said to Suzanne, as they took seats in the back of the bus.

"That would be so cool," Suzanne agreed. "We could teach everyone how to build a fire."

Just then, Katie felt someone knocking on the window beside her. It was Genie.

Katie opened the window. "Thanks so much," she said. "I really learned a lot."

Genie grinned. "So did I. I learned that kids can do a whole lot for themselves . . . if you give them the chance."

As the bus drove off, Katie felt a cool breeze blow on her through the open window. She was pretty sure it wasn't a magic wind. But she reached up and shut the window— just in case.

No sense taking any chances.

Chapter 14

Science Camp definitely was a fun time. The nature arts counselor had lots of great ideas for nature projects the kids could do. Everyone in class 3A came home with natural soaps that they made all by themselves.

You can make your own Science Camp soap on a rope. Here's how.

Soap on a Rope
You will need:
3 cups Ivory Snow detergent or other
 soap flakes
bowl
liquid food coloring

1 cup water

vegetable oil

a thin piece of rope

Here's what you do: Pour the soap flakes into a bowl. Put a few drops of food coloring in the water. Pour the water onto the soap flakes. Use your hands to mix the contents of the bowl until they feel like clay or dough. Massage a drop or two of vegetable oil into the palms of your hands. Now shape the soap anyway you like. Tie the ends of the rope together. Gently push the knotted end of the rope into your finished soap shape. Let the soap stand overnight to set.

KATIE KAZOO, SWITCHEROO

Drat! You Copycat!

by Nancy Krulik • illustrated by John & Wendy

Grosset & Dunlap

For Mandy and Ian—N.K.

Library of Congress Cataloging-in-Publication Data

Krulik, Nancy E.
    Drat! You copycat! / by Nancy Krulik ; illustrated by John & Wendy.
        p. cm.—(Katie Kazoo, switcheroo ; 7)
Summary: Katie agrees to be a buddy for the new girl in class even though her best friend Suzanne does not approve.
    [1. First day of school—Fiction. 2. Moving, Household—Fiction. 3. Schools—Fiction. 4. Magic—Fiction.] I. John & Wendy, ill. II. Title.
    PZ7.K944Dr 2003
    [Fic]—dc21

                                                    2003005965

            ISBN 0-448-43171-8   I J

—

Chapter 1

"Boys and girls, say hello to Becky Stern," Mrs. Derkman told class 3A .

It was early Monday morning. The teacher was standing in the front of the classroom. Beside her was a small girl with a long, blond ponytail.

"Hi, Becky," the kids all said at once.

"Becky and her family have just moved here from Atlanta. I know you will all try to make her feel welcome," Mrs. Derkman said.

The class stared at Becky. Becky stared back at the class. Her blue eyes were wide open. Her face was pale. She looked really scared.

Katie Carew raised her hand.

"Yes Katie?" Mrs. Derkman replied.

"Who is going to be Becky's buddy?"

Jeremy Fox, one of Katie's best friends, smiled proudly when Katie said that. It had been his idea to give new students a buddy when they started at school. That way they'd have a friend right away.

"Well, Katie," Mrs. Derkman said, "would you like to be Becky's buddy?"

Katie grinned. "Sure."

"Becky, stick with Katie this week. She'll show you around. Now take a seat at the empty desk in the second row." Mrs. Derkman said.

All eyes were on Becky as she sat down.

"Okay, everyone," Mrs. Derkman announced. "Please pull out your vocabulary notebooks and copy down this week's word list."

As Katie opened her notebook, a tightly folded piece of paper landed on her desk. She

hoped Mrs. Derkman hadn't seen that.

Mrs. Derkman hated it when kids passed notes. Sometimes she even read the notes out loud. That could be very embarrassing.

But right now, Mrs. Derkman had her back turned to the class. She hadn't seen a thing. *Phew*. Katie quickly unfolded the paper.

The note was from Suzanne. "Why did you say you would be her buddy? We were supposed to play double dutch with Miriam and Zoe today. The new girl is wearing a

dress. She can't jump rope in a dress. All the boys will see her underpants."

Katie wasn't sure what to write back. Suzanne's note was kind of mean. It wasn't like Katie had been trying to ruin Suzanne's recess. She was just trying to help the new girl.

But Suzanne was one of Katie's best friends. Katie didn't want her to be mad. She quickly scribbled back an answer. "Becky's new. I was just trying to be nice. Maybe we can all do something else instead."

Just then, Mrs. Derkman turned to face the class. Katie quickly shoved the paper into her desk.

"Okay, class, our first vocabulary word is *bauble*," Mrs. Derkman said. "Can anyone use it in a sentence?"

"I got one," George Brennan shouted out from his seat in the front row. "When I really stink, I take a *bauble* bath!"

Everyone started laughing—everyone

except Mrs. Derkman, anyway.

Mrs. Derkman shook her head. "George, that's not how we behave in class. I don't want to have to talk to you again," she warned sternly. The teacher turned to the rest of the class. "A bauble is a small trinket. Now, does anyone else have a sentence?"

Suzanne raised her hand high.

"Yes, Suzanne," Mrs. Derkman said.

Suzanne sat up straight and smiled as everyone looked at her. "To a princess, an emerald necklace is just a bauble," she said.

Katie choked back a laugh. Somehow, Suzanne always found a way to talk about jewelry, makeup, or fashion.

"Very nice, Suzanne," Mrs. Derkman said. "Anyone else have a sentence?"

Becky shyly raised her hand.

"Okay, Becky," Mrs. Derkman said.

"To Queen Elizabeth, a diamond ring is just a bauble," Becky said in her slow, Southern accent.

"That's just like what you said," Kevin whispered to Suzanne.

Suzanne didn't answer him. She just stared at her own bauble—a plastic diamond ring she wore on her finger.

Katie didn't like vocabulary very much. She liked reading and history a lot more.

Before she knew it, her notebook page was filled with all sorts of doodles. Katie always drew when she got bored.

It seemed like forever until Mrs. Derkman looked at the clock that hung over the classroom doorway. "It's time for lunch," she said finally. "Let's line up."

"All right!" shouted Kevin. "Tomato time!"

"What's he talking about?" Becky asked softly, as she walked over to where Katie and Suzanne were standing.

Katie grinned. "You'll see," she said. "Lunchtime is always tomato time for Kevin."

Becky forced a nervous smile to her lips. "Thanks for saying you'd be my buddy this week," she said in her thick Southern accent. "I hope I'm not getting in the way of anything y'all wanted to do."

Suzanne glanced over at the two double-Dutch jump ropes Miriam was carrying down to the lunchroom for recess. "Well, as a matter of fact . . ." she began.

But Katie didn't let Suzanne finish. She knew whatever Suzanne said would hurt Becky's feelings. Suzanne sometimes said mean things. It wasn't that Suzanne wasn't nice. She just didn't always think before she spoke.

Becky hadn't had a chance to see Suzanne's good side—the side of her that was fun and exciting, and made you feel important just because you were her friend. Katie wanted Becky to know that Suzanne was really a good person.

"She's just kidding," Katie assured Becky. "We can all play together. Suzanne's great at coming up with fun stuff to do."

Suzanne glared at Katie.

Katie ignored her.

"Come on," Katie urged Becky. "Let's go to the cafeteria. I want to get there before all the chocolate pudding is gone."

Chapter 2

Katie showed Becky where the lunch line was in the cafeteria. She helped her get a tray and pick out her food.

Once the girls paid for their lunches, they carried their trays over to a table near the windows. Suzanne was already sitting there with Miriam Chan, Mandy Banks, and some of the other kids in class 3A .

Becky took a seat beside Katie. She smiled at Suzanne. Suzanne barely even glanced in Becky's direction. Instead she opened her pink and purple lunch bag. Inside was a small plastic container. Suzanne tore off the lid and showed everyone a strange-looking mix of

rice, lentil beans, and tomato sauce.

Manny Gonzalez looked across the table at Suzanne's lunch. "Ooh! Gross!" he shouted. He made a grunting noise. "I think I'm gonna puke!"

Suzanne rolled her eyes. "That shows what you know. This is *kosheri*. It's a recipe from Egypt. I'll bet Cleopatra ate it."

"Oh no, here we go again," Manny moaned.

Becky looked curiously at Katie.

"Suzanne is crazy about Cleopatra," Katie explained to her.

"It's all she's talked about for the past two weeks," Manny said.

"That's better than last month, when all she talked about was that artist, Vincent van Gogh," Mandy told Becky.

"She kept telling us how he chopped his ear off," Katie said. "Yuck."

"You're lucky. Hearing about Cleopatra's better than that," Mandy assured Becky.

"Cleopatra was better than anyone," Suzanne insisted. "She was the most powerful woman in ancient Egypt. She was . . ."

"The Queen of the Nile," Katie, Miriam, Mandy, and Manny all finished her sentence for her. They'd heard Suzanne give the same Cleopatra speech about a gazillion times in the past two weeks.

"Well, I don't care who ate that stuff. It's gross," Manny said. "It looks like something George would do with his food."

Katie looked over at George. He'd already begun mixing his spaghetti into his chocolate

pudding. George always made a mess of his food. Then he'd wait for someone to dare him to eat it—which he always did.

George cracked Katie up. He told the best jokes. Nothing was too wild or too weird for him to try.

George had also been the one to give Katie her nickname, Katie Kazoo. It sounded a lot like Katie Carew, only cooler. Katie loved it!

Just then, Kevin and Jeremy came over to the table. Kevin's tray was stacked high with tomatoes—round cherry tomatoes, small grape tomatoes, and thick, beefy tomato slices.

"Okay guys, it's tomato time!" Kevin announced happily.

Everyone watched as Jeremy threw one of Kevin's cherry tomatoes up in the air. Kevin opened his mouth wide—and caught it easily. Some of the kids clapped. Kevin took a bow and chomped away.

"Kevin's going for the world record," Katie

explained to Becky. "He's already eaten two hundred thirty-seven tomatoes this month!"

"I love tomatoes," Becky interrupted. She smiled at Kevin. "One time I ate a tomato this big." She held her arms in a circle the size of a pumpkin.

Kevin rolled his eyes. "Tomatoes don't grow that big," he told her, "not even prize-winning ones. You can't fool me. I know all about tomatoes. I've read books on them and everything."

Becky blushed tomato red.

Suzanne didn't want to discuss tomatoes. She wasn't finished talking about Cleopatra.

"You know, I asked my mother to get me a cat," she told the other girls.

"Did she say yes?" Katie asked excitedly. "It's so great having a pet. You know how much fun Pepper and I have together." Pepper was Katie's chocolate-brown-and-white cocker spaniel. She adored him.

"Well a cat is different than a dog," Suzanne said. "I mean, dogs are fun and all, but cats are smart. The ancient Egyptians worshipped them—even Cleopatra."

"*Pepper's* smart," Katie insisted. "I taught him a new trick the other day. When I hold up a treat, he dances on his hind legs."

"Pepper *is* smart," Suzanne assured her best friend. "For a dog, anyway," she added under her breath.

"I used to have a dog," Becky told Katie. She turned to Suzanne. "But now I have a cat.

Her name's Fluffy. She's white and cuddly. And she's *really* smart." She turned to Suzanne and smiled. "Maybe you'll want to come over and play with her one day."

Suzanne ate a forkful of lentil beans.

"Hey Kevin, what do you call a pet tomato?" George asked.

"What?" Kevin asked between bites of a tomato wedge. Red tomato juice dribbled out of his mouth and onto his chin.

"Call it anything you want," George laughed. "It can't hear you!"

Jeremy laughed so hard at George's joke that milk came out of his nose.

George smiled. "Jeremy, you're the best audience. You'll laugh at anything."

Becky looked at Jeremy and smiled. "I know a good joke," she told him.

Suzanne rolled her eyes. "I'm finished eating," she said, before Becky could tell her joke. "Let's go play double Dutch."

"I love double Dutch," Becky said. "Back

in Atlanta we used to have contests to see who could jump the longest without missing. I was always the winner."

Miriam, Mandy, and Zoe Canter were impressed.

Suzanne wasn't. She turned to Becky. "I'd ask you to play, but you're wearing a dress . . . unless you've got shorts under there."

Becky shook her head. "I never thought to do that."

"All the girls in our class wear shorts underneath their dresses," Zoe told her. "That way you can play and no one sees your underpants."

"Wow!" Becky exclaimed.

"It was Suzanne's idea," Miriam said.

"Suzanne is definitely the fashion expert around here," Katie agreed.

Suzanne laughed. "Everyone needs a hobby."

Becky looked at Suzanne's leopard-print shirt. It had fake fur on the cuffs. Her pants were glittery-black.

Katie had hoped Suzanne would have wanted to do something else at recess. But it was clear that wasn't going to happen. Sometimes Suzanne could be so stubborn.

But Katie didn't want to argue with her in front of everyone. That would just make Becky feel bad. "You guys go ahead and jump rope," she told the others, finally. "Becky and I can do something else. Maybe play foursquare."

"It's okay, Katie," Becky said. "If you want to jump rope, I can just watch for today."

"No way," Katie told Becky. "There's always lots of fun stuff going on during recess."

Katie smiled warmly at Becky. But the new girl wasn't looking in Katie's direction. She was busy watching Suzanne's sparkly silver sneakers move back and forth as Suzanne walked away.

Chapter 3

The next morning, Katie was the first kid to arrive at Cherrydale Elementary School. She wanted to be there before Becky arrived. Katie took the job of being Becky's school buddy very seriously.

She sat down on a woooden bench and looked around nervously. It was creepy being the only one on the playground. Everything was so quiet . . . and lonely.

Katie didn't like being alone. Lately it seemed as though whenever she was all by herself, strange things happened.

It had all started a few weeks ago on one really horrible day. Katie had lost the football

game for her team. She'd fallen in the mud and ruined her favorite jeans. Then, as if all that weren't bad enough, Katie had burped really loudly in front of the whole class!

The day had been so incredibly, unbelievably awful that Katie had wished she could be anyone but herself. There must have been a shooting star flying overhead or something, because the very next day the magic wind came.

The magic wind was like no wind Katie had seen before. It was a wild, fierce tornado that only blew around Katie.

But the tornado-like gusts weren't the worst part of the magic wind.

The worst part came *after* the wind had stopped blowing. That's when the magic wind turned Katie into someone else.

The magic wind could turn Katie into anyone! One time it transformed her into Suzanne's baby sister, Heather. Suzanne had almost changed Katie's diaper! How

embarrassing would *that* have been?

But even that wasn't as bad as the time the wind turned her into Jeremy Fox. Katie didn't know anything about being a boy!

Katie knew the magic wind wasn't through with her yet. It could show up at any time—as long as no one but Katie was around.

"Hey, Katie Kazoo, you're here early," George called out as he rode his skateboard onto the playground.

Katie was glad someone else had arrived.

"Skateboarding is so cool!" George exclaimed. "That's why I'm doing my research

project on the history of skateboarding."

Katie gulped. The research project! Katie had been so excited about being Becky's buddy that she'd forgotten to think of a topic.

"What are you going to research?" George asked her.

"Well, I . . . uh . . ." Katie stammered. Out of the corner of her eye, she spotted the picture frame key chain on her backpack. It had a photo of her dog in it.

"I'm going to do my research project about cocker spaniels," Katie blurted out.

Phew. Pepper didn't know it, but he had just saved Katie.

"That doesn't sound like too *ruff* of a topic," George teased her. "You should be able to find a lot of information *fur* your paper."

"Maybe Mrs. Derkman will let me bring Pepper in as an example," Katie said.

George shook his head. "Are you nuts? Mrs. Derkman doesn't even like having Speedy in the classroom. And he's just a hamster. How

do you think she'd feel about a dog?"

Katie nodded. "You're right. I'll bring in some pictures."

Just then, Suzanne wandered onto the playground. It was impossible not to notice her. She was wearing a hot pink glittery rugby shirt. Her capri pants were hot pink and covered in glitter, too.

"New outfit?" Katie asked her.

Suzanne nodded. "Yes! It's so me!"

Katie nodded. "No one likes glitter as much as you do!"

"So, what are you doing for your project?" George interrupted. He didn't want to sit there talking about clothes with two girls.

"Well, I . . ." Suzanne began. But before she could finish her sentence, she saw something terrible heading toward the playground. "Oh, no!" she cried out.

"What is it?" Katie asked.

Suzanne was too upset to speak. She just reached out her hand and pointed.

Katie gasped. It was Becky!

She was wearing a leopard-print shirt with fake fur at the cuffs.

Her pants were glittery-black.

It was the exact same outfit Suzanne had worn yesterday.

No one in class 3A had ever bought one of Suzanne's outfits before. They wouldn't dare.

"This is just horrible!" Suzanne moaned.

Chapter 4

Katie walked quietly into room 3A. She hung up her jacket, dropped her homework in the bin, and sat down at her desk. One second later, a note landed on her desk.

The note was from Suzanne. Katie glanced over at her best friend. She'd been really brave to pass the note just then. Mrs. Derkman hadn't even turned her back to the class.

Obviously Suzanne was so angry at Becky, she didn't care if she caught.

Katie slipped the note under her desk and quietly opened the paper. Suzanne's writing was big, thick, and dark. There were only four words on the paper.

BECKY IS A COPYCAT!

Katie took out her pink pen and scribbled an answer to Suzanne's note.

"Maybe she didn't know you always wear glitter," she wrote.

"Kevin," Katie whispered. "Could you pass this to Suzanne?"

Kevin sat, right between Katie and Suzanne. "I'm not getting in trouble," he said.

Katie sighed. It was too dangerous for her to throw the note to Suzanne. If Mrs. Derkman read this note out loud, Becky's feelings would be hurt.

"I'll give you my dessert at lunch if you'll pass the note," she whispered quickly.

Kevin thought for a moment. "And the tomatoes from your salad, too?" he asked.

Katie nodded.

Kevin quickly snatched the note from Katie's hand and slipped it to Suzanne.

Katie watched as Suzanne unfolded the paper. Suzanne frowned, and shook her head.

"Whose side are you on?" she hissed over Kevin's head.

"I'm not on anyone's side," Katie whispered back.

"Girls!" Mrs. Derkman said sternly. "Is there something you want to share with the entire class?"

For one scary moment, Katie thought Suzanne might call Becky a copycat in front everyone. But Suzanne didn't say anything. She just sat up tall and glared at the back of Becky's head.

"Okay then," Mrs. Derkman said. "Let's get to work. The first thing I want to discuss are your topics for your research papers." "Let's begin with the first row."

George sat in the first seat in the first row. Mrs. Derkman had put him there so she could

keep an eye on him. "I'm doing a paper on skateboarding," George told her. "It will be *wheel-y* exciting."

A few of the kids groaned at George's bad joke. Mrs. Derkman never even looked up. She just wrote George's topic in her notebook. "Okay, how about you, Mandy?"

"I want to do a research paper on dragonflies. We have a lot of them living near the creek behind my house," Mandy answered.

"That will be very nice," Mrs. Derkman said. "Just please don't bring any of them into the classroom."

Everybody laughed. They all knew that Mrs. Derkman was very afraid of bugs.

"And you, Jeremy?" Mrs. Derkman asked.

"I want to do a report on soccer," Jeremy said. "It's my favorite sport."

"Just remember, you can't play ball in the classroom," Mrs. Derkman reminded him.

"I'm going to make a videotape," Jeremy assured her.

Mrs. Derkman smiled. "That's a fine idea. Okay, now let's move on to the second row. Have you come up with something, Becky?"

Becky sat up very straight and tall. "I want to do my research project on Cleopatra," she said.

The class was silent.

They couldn't believe their ears. Everyone figured Suzanne would be the one to do a research project about Cleopatra. The kids all turned around to see how Suzanne was taking the news: *not* well.

Suzanne's eyes were closed in angry little slits. Her mouth was clenched tightly. She was obviously really mad—so mad, in fact, that she forgot Mrs. Derkman's rule about calling out.

"That's my topic!" Suzanne shouted. "I was going to do Cleopatra! Everybody knew it."

Becky shook her head. "I didn't know it."

Suzanne glared at her. "Yes you did. You knew how I felt about Cleopatra. You heard

me talking about her at lunch. Becky, you're a
great big copycat!"

The class gasped. No one had ever acted
that way in Mrs. Derkman's room before. Not
even George.

"Suzanne Lock," Mrs. Derkman said
sternly. "That is *not* how we behave in class.
Becky will be doing a report on Cleopatra.
You will have to find another topic to
research. There are lots of interesting people
or things you can learn about."

"Not as interesting as Cleopatra," Suzanne
moaned.

Mrs. Derkman sighed. "Oh, I think there are. In fact, I'm going to give you a topic for your project. You will do a report on Coco Chanel."

"What's a Coco Chanel?" Suzanne demanded. "Some sort of candy bar?"

Mrs. Derkman laughed. "No. Coco Chanel was a person. A very special person."

"Why?" Suzanne asked.

"You'll see," Mrs. Derkman said, as she wrote the topic in her book. She smiled at Suzanne. "I promise that you—of all people—will find her very interesting."

Suzanne sat back, folded her arms, and stared furiously at Becky.

Katie gulped. She'd seen that look on Suzanne's face before. *I'm sure glad I'm not Becky,* she thought to herself.

Chapter 5

"Now do you believe me? I told you Becky was a copycat!" Suzanne insisted, as she and Katie walked out of the school building at the end of the day.

Katie nodded slowly. She couldn't defend Becky anymore. Taking Suzanne's research topic had been really mean.

"I can't believe Mrs. Derkman is making me do a research project on that Coco Chanel person," Suzanne moaned. "I don't even know who she is."

"You can come over to my house and we can look her up on the Internet," Katie suggested.

Suzanne shrugged. "Why not? At least I'll

be able to eat some of your mom's cookies while we work."

Katie grinned. Her mom did bake great cookies. Suzanne's mother usually served the store-bought kind.

Just then, Becky came running up to the girls. "Are y'all going to the library to start

your research?" she asked in her soft Southern accent.

Katie was about to tell Becky that she and Suzanne were going to her house to use the computer, but Suzanne shot Katie one of her don't-you-dare looks.

Becky looked hopefully at Katie. That made Katie feel terrible. She was supposed to be Becky's buddy, and she wasn't inviting her to come along. Katie knew Becky was feeling left out.

But Suzanne's feelings had been hurt, too. She needed Katie every bit as much as Becky did. Katie didn't know what to do.

Suzanne solved that problem for her.

"We have other plans," Suzanne told Becky simply. "You'll have to float down the Nile without us."

Becky looked curiously at Suzanne.

"The Nile," Suzanne repeated. "That's a river in Egypt. You'd have known that if you were as big a fan of Cleopatra as I am."

Becky smiled. "I'm going to learn all about Cleopatra. Then you and I can talk about her. Maybe we can even start a Cleopatra club."

"Whatever." Suzanne sighed. She put her thumbs together and held her pointer fingers straight up to make a big W.

This was going to get ugly—Katie could tell. She quickly grabbed Suzanne by the elbow. "We've got to go. See you tomorrow, Becky."

"I don't believe that girl!" Suzanne exclaimed, as she and Katie walked off. "A Cleopatra club? How could she?"

"She just wants to be friends." Katie said.

Suzanne rolled her eyes. "I'd rather be friends with a three-headed rat."

Katie sighed. There was no point in arguing with Suzanne when she was this angry. It was easier to change the topic. "You can use the Internet first," she told her. "I have a book on cocker spaniels that I can start with."

Before long, the girls had reached Katie's

house. Mrs. Carew was sitting on the front steps with Pepper when they arrived.

"Hi, girls," she greeted them. "How was school?"

"Rotten," Suzanne moaned.

"Fine," Katie said at the exact same time.

Mrs. Carew laughed. "Are you sure you were in the same classroom?" She held out a plate of warm sugar cookies with M&M's baked into them.

"The new girl stole my research topic," Suzanne explained between cookie bites. "Katie got the topic she wanted."

"Cocker spaniels," Katie told her mother.

Mrs. Carew laughed as Katie scratched Pepper behind the ears. "Of course," she said.

"I wanted to do Cleopatra. But Blechy Becky is researching her," Suzanne said. "Mrs. Derkman is making me do a report on some lady named Coco Chanel."

"Oh, you're going to love Coco!" Katie's mom exclaimed. "She's very interesting."

Suzanne made a face.

"Besides, you already know everything there is to know about Cleopatra," Mrs. Carew said. "Now you'll learn something new."

Katie and Suzanne looked at each other. That was one of those things only a grown-up would say. You couldn't argue with it—even though you wished you could.

"Let's go find out who this Coco Chanel lady is," Katie told Suzanne.

Suzanne nodded and followed Katie into the living room. The girls sat down and booted up the computer. Suzanne typed the words

"Coco Chanel" into the search engine. Almost instantly the link to a short biography appeared on the screen.

Coco Chanel: This French fashion designer's real name was Gabrielle Chanel. Coco Chanel changed fashion forever. She designed the first pants for women. She was famous for wearing lots of beads and carrying quilted pocketbooks with chains. She also created perfumes.

"Oooh! Katie, look at her," Suzanne squealed, pointing to the photograph.

Katie looked at the picture of a dark-haired woman in a black pantsuit. She wore strands and strands of white pearls around her neck. She looked very elegant.

"Isn't she wonderful?" Suzanne asked Katie. "Don't you just love all those beads? Do you think I should wear my hair short like that?"

Katie laughed. Good-bye Cleo, Hello Coco.

Chapter 6

"Teddy bear, teddy bear, turn around. Teddy bear, teddy bear, touch the ground," Becky chanted as she jumped over the two double-Dutch jump ropes.

Becky, Miriam, and Zoe were already playing in the schoolyard when Katie arrived the next morning. Katie walked over to watch.

"Teddy bear, teddy bear, touch your toe," Becky continued as she tapped her foot with her hand. "Teddy bear, teddy bear, out you go!" she shouted as she dashed out from between the twirling ropes.

"That was great!" Miriam congratulated Becky. "You didn't miss once."

Becky smiled and looked over at Katie. "Hi! Where's Suzanne?"

Katie shrugged. "We don't usually walk to school together. Why?" After what had happened yesterday, Katie couldn't believe that Becky would be looking for Suzanne.

"I just thought she'd like to jump double Dutch with me. I know a whole bunch of jump-rope rhymes."

Katie didn't think Suzanne would want to learn any of Becky's rhymes, but she didn't tell Becky that. Instead, she said, "Nice outfit. Is it new?"

Becky was wearing a purple shirt with a pink flower in the center. The shirt matched her purple glittery skirt perfectly.

"I found it at the mall," Becky told her. "I thought it was really cool." She lifted her skirt a little. "And see, I'm wearing shorts."

"Do you want to jump again, Becky?" Zoe interrupted. "Since you didn't miss, you get another turn."

"Okay," Becky said. As Miriam and Zoe began turning the ropes, Becky leaped in. "Fortune-teller if you're so smart, tell me the name of my sweetheart. Is it A . . . B . . . C . . ."

Becky kept jumping, twirling around as she said each letter. The ropes were moving at a very steady rhythm, until suddenly . . .

"Look at Suzanne!" Zoe cried out. She dropped one of her ropes. Instantly, Becky

tripped over the fallen jump rope. "Hey! Why did you stop turning?" she asked.

But there was no one around to answer her. Miriam and Zoe were both running over to meet Suzanne at the far end of the playground.

"Wow, Suzanne! You look great," Mandy Banks exclaimed. "I love those beads."

Suzanne fingered the many strands of white plastic beads she wore around her neck. She smoothed the creases in her black slacks and straightened her plain black shirt.

Katie was amazed. The girls had only seen the picture of Coco Chanel yesterday. And Suzanne was already dressed like her.

"Hey there, Coco," Katie teased.

"Don't you just love this outfit?" Suzanne gushed. "My mom helped me put it together. She's so glad that I'm over all that glitter stuff." Suzanne stared at Becky's outfit.

Just then George and Jeremy wandered over to see what all the fuss was about.

"What are you supposed to be?" Jeremy asked.

"Let me check my calendar," George said. "I think I missed Halloween."

Suzanne rolled her eyes. "You boys don't know anything. This outfit is very grown-up."

"But you're not a grown-up, Suzanne," Jeremy reminded her. "How are you going to play any games in that getup?"

"Maybe I don't feel like playing games," Suzanne argued.

"What are you going to do at recess then?"

"I'm going to spend recess drawing clothes," she told him.

George made a face. "Boring!" he said.

"No, it's not!" Suzanne replied. "I can get lots of ideas for new fashions here. As Coco Chanel said, 'Fashion is in the air. Born upon the wind.' "

George and Jeremy had no idea what Suzanne was talking about.

"Forget Coco Chanel," George moaned.

"You're *Cuckoo* Chanel."

Jeremy laughed. "See ya later, Cuckoo," he said as he ran off toward the soccer field.

"Cuckoo, cuckoo," George added, sounding very much like a cuckoo clock.

As soon as the boys were gone, Becky held up a her purple lunch bag. "I brought lunch today," she told Suzanne. "It's pita bread and bean salad. I've got dried figs for dessert. I thought we could share our lunches and have an Egyptian feast."

Suzanne shook her head. "Sorry, Becky. I have French bread and a hunk of cheese for lunch today. That's what they eat in Paris. Coco Chanel lived in Paris, you know."

Becky bit her lip. "Oh. Well, bread and cheese sounds good, too."

"It is," Suzanne assured her. "I love everything that's French. As far as I'm concerned, Egypt is ancient history!"

Chapter 7

"Look at Blechy Becky," Suzanne said as she watched Becky drag a huge black duffel bag to her desk. It had been two weeks since Becky had chosen Cleopatra as her research topic, but Suzanne still didn't like her.

"What do you think she has in there?" Mandy wondered.

"Maybe a mummy," Suzanne joked. "That would be perfect. After all, only a *dead person* would hang around with her."

"That's really mean, Suzanne," Katie said.

"Not as mean as copying my clothes and stealing my research topic," Suzanne said.

"She's probably got the stuff for her report

in that bag," Katie said.

Today was the first day of the research project presentations. Two kids would give speeches each day. George and Becky were first.

"She sure doesn't look like Cleopatra," Suzanne said, staring at Becky's white blouse, black stretch jeans, and chunky red beads. "The Queen of the Nile didn't wear beads. Coco Chanel wore beads. *I* wear beads. She's not trying to be like Cleopatra. She's trying to be like me. She's such a wanna-be."

Before Katie could say a word, Mrs. Derkman stood in front of the room. "Will everyone sit down, please?" she said.

The kids quickly scrambled to their seats.

"We're going to get started on our research presentations," the teacher continued. "George, do you want to go first?"

Katie glanced over at George. He was wearing baggy orange shorts and a huge yellow-and-orange Hawaiian shirt. He was

also wearing his helmet and pads. He certainly looked ready to go first.

"Sure!" George exclaimed. He walked to the front of the room and held up his skateboard. "Hey there, dudes and honeys. This is my stick."

Mrs. Derkman looked curiously at George. "Excuse me?"

George laughed. "All I said was, 'Hi everyone. This is my board.' I was using surfing slang."

"I thought your report was about skateboarding," Manny interrupted.

"It is," George said. "Skateboarding became really popular in the 1950s. Back then, everyone in California was surfing. Other kids wanted to surf, too. But not everyone lived near an ocean. So skateboards were great. You could catch the surfing wave no matter where you lived. That's why a lot of skateboarding words sound like surfer words."

George put one foot on the back of his

skateboard. "I'm going to show you a cool skateboarding move," he told the class. "It's called Mondo Foot."

Mondo foot? Katie couldn't help it. She started to giggle. So did lots of other kids.

"No, really," George told them. "When you do Mondo Foot, you push the board with your front foot, like this."

George pushed off with his front foot. His skateboard soared across the floor.

Unfortunately, George wasn't on the skateboard. He'd slipped off. *Crash!* The board slammed into the trash can. Trash spilled out all over the floor.

George leaped across the room to grab his board. As he ran, he tripped over the fallen trash can. George went flying through the air. He landed headfirst right on top of Katie's desk.

George was lucky he was wearing a helmet.

Too bad Katie wasn't. George slammed right into her face.

"Ouch!" Katie shouted, as she grabbed her nose.

"I'm sorry," George mumbled. He looked embarrassed.

"It's okay," Katie told him. "I'm alright."

But Katie *wasn't* alright. Her nose was bleeding.

"Oooh! Yuck!" Kevin shouted when he saw the red blood running from Katie's nose. He moved his chair far from Katie.

Mrs. Derkman walked over and handed Katie a wad of tissues. "It's just a little blood,

Kevin," she said. "Katie, go to the nurse and get an ice pack. George, finish your report without any more demonstrations, alright?"

"Okay," George said. He sounded disappointed.

Katie held the tissues tightly against her nose as she headed out of the room and down the long, empty hallway to the nurse's office. She was determined not to get any blood on her shirt.

Suddenly, Katie felt a cool wind blowing on the back of her neck. She quickly looked around. There were no windows in the hallway, and the doors were all shut tight.

Katie gulped. This was no ordinary wind. This was the magic wind!

The magic wind began spinning faster and faster all around Katie. Her red hair whipped wildly around her head.

Katie shut her eyes tightly, and tried not to cry. As the fierce tornado swirled, she grabbed onto a locker.

And then it stopped. Just like that. No
warning. But Katie wasn't surprised. The
magic wind never gave her any warning. In
fact, it never felt the same way twice. The
magic wind was always different—as different
as the people it turned Katie into.

Which brought up the big question: Just
who had the magic wind turned Katie into
this time?

Chapter 8

Katie was afraid to open her eyes. She had no idea where she was. All she knew was that she was sitting, and she used to be standing.

Suddenly, Katie heard loud applause. Where was she? A theater? A ball game?

Slowly, Katie let her eyes flutter open.

"Oh my goodness," she muttered to herself. "How did I wind up here?"

Somehow, Katie had come back to class 3A. Everyone was sitting happily in their seats. George was standing in the front of the room, taking a bow.

"That was very good, George," Mrs. Derkman said, as she walked to the front of

the room. "We have all learned a lot about skateboarding."

"And about skate*falling*," Manny teased.

George blushed.

"Okay, please take your seat, George," Mrs. Derkman said. "Now we will hear all about Cleopatra. It's your turn, Becky."

Suddenly, all eyes turned to look at Katie. Katie stared back at her classmates.

"Becky?" Mrs. Derkman said. She walked over to where Katie was sitting.

Slowly, Katie looked down. Instead of her own faded jeans and blue shirt, Katie was wearing a white blouse, black stretch jeans, and big red beads.

Katie gulped as she wiped a strand of blond hair from her eyes. Oh, no! Katie had turned into Becky. Mrs. Derkman expected her to give a report, but Katie didn't know anything about Cleopatra.

"Becky, it's your turn," Mrs. Derkman coaxed sternly.

Katie didn't know what to do. If she didn't go up in front of the classroom right now, Becky would get an *F* on her report.

Katie couldn't let *that* happen.

But she couldn't teach the class anything about Cleopatra, either.

Then Katie remembered the black bag Becky had dragged to school that day. It was sitting right at her feet. Maybe there was something in the bag that could help her give the report.

"Okay, Mrs. Derkman," Katie said as she unzipped the bag. Her voice sounded so strange. It had the same soft, singsongy Southern accent as the real Becky's.

Slowly, Katie peered into the bag. The first thing she spotted was a package of note cards.

Phew. Becky had written out her speech on the cards.

Then Katie pulled out a black wig and a huge hat with some sort of snake on the top.

Under that was a long, clingy, white dress. There was a stuffed cat in the bag as well.

Quickly, Katie threw the costume on over Becky's everyday clothes. She picked up the cat and the cards, and walked to the front of the room.

Immediately Suzanne started laughing. "Her crown's on backward," She giggled. "The snake's supposed to go in the front!"

"Suzanne!" Mrs. Derkman warned.

Suzanne stopped her giggling right away.

Katie blushed and turned the crown around. Then she looked at the notecards in her hand. They were very hard to read. Becky did not have neat handwriting.

"Cleopatra was born in Egypt in 69 B.C.," Katie began slowly, as she struggled to understand Becky's notes. "She was famous for her beauty."

Katie looked out at the kids in her class. They seemed interested. Well, at least everyone other than Suzanne seemed interested. Things weren't going too badly. She turned to the next card.

"Cleopatra was the daughter of King . . ."

But before Katie could finish her sentence, she lost her grip on the notecards. The the whole pile slipped from her hands.

"Oops!" Katie exclaimed. Quickly, she bent down to scoop up Becky's cards. As she looked down at the cards, the Cleopatra

crown fell from Katie's head. The black wig slipped down over her eyes. Katie could barely see past the long dark hair. And as if that weren't bad enough . . .

Rrrip. Becky's long white dress ripped right up the back. Everyone heard the dress tear.

"Boy, Cleopatra must have been a klutz!" George joked.

"This is too funny!" Suzanne began to giggle. So did a lot of other kids.

Katie could feel her face turning red with embarrassment.

"Class!" Mrs. Derkman scolded. "Show Becky the same respect you would like to be shown during your report."

Mrs. Derkman sounded really angry. Instantly, the class got quiet. They waited for Becky to speak.

But the note cards were all out of order now. Katie had no idea what she was supposed to say next. This report was turning into a disaster!

Katie looked out at her classmates. They were all sitting silently, waiting for her to say something.

Quickly, Katie read whatever was written on the card at the top of her pile. "Cleopatra was absolutely crazy about Caesar," she told the class.

"About who?" Manny asked.

"Caesar," Katie repeated.

"Caesar who?" Manny asked.

Katie had no idea. "Um . . . Caesar . . .

Caesar . . . uh . . . Caesar salad." she blurted out finally.

Everyone began laughing again.

Katie thought she was going to cry.

"I think you mean *Julius* Caesar," Suzanne told her. "He was a famous Roman general. Everyone knows that."

Not everyone, Katie thought miserably.

Suzanne started to giggle again. Soon everyone else was laughing, too.

Katie couldn't take it anymore. She ran out of the classroom in tears.

As she raced down the empty hallway, Katie could hear the kids in room 3A making fun of Becky's speech. She could also hear Mrs. Derkman ordering her to come back.

But Katie wasn't going back into that room.

At least not as long as she was Becky Stern.

Chapter 9

Katie ran into the bathroom to wash her face. She couldn't let anyone see her with blotchy skin and red eyes. It was bad enough that she'd ruined Becky's report. She couldn't let everyone think she was a big crybaby, too.

Katie turned on the cold water and put her hands under the faucet. Right away, she felt a draft blowing on her neck.

Katie looked over at the bathroom windows. They were locked tightly. And the door hadn't opened since Katie had walked into the room. Quickly Katie bent down and peered under the two bathroom stalls. There was no one in either one.

Katie was all alone in the girls bathroom.

The magic wind only came when Katie was alone.

Katie grabbed on to the and held on tightly. She knew what was coming next. That breeze was about to become a tornado!

Sure enough, within seconds, wild winds began to swirl all around Katie. This time, the wind was bitter and cold. Katie could feel goosebumps popping up all over her body as the gusts churned around her.

And then it was all over. Just like that. The air was still, and the bathroom was warm again.

Nervously, Katie looked into the bathroom mirror. Her own face stared back at her. She could see her own red hair and the freckles across her nose. Katie Kazoo was back!

And so was Becky. In fact, she was standing right next to Katie, wearing a crooked wig and a ripped white dress, looking confused.

"How did I get in here?" she asked Katie.

"Don't you remember?" Katie replied.

"Well, sort of. I think I was giving my report, but I'm not sure. It's all kind of fuzzy."

Katie gulped. How was she going to explain this? She couldn't just come out and say that she had turned into Becky and given her report for her. Becky would never believe her. Katie wouldn't have believed it, either—if it hadn't happened to her.

"My report was a real mess," Becky moaned. "I'm not sure what happened. It's like it was me up there in front of everyone, but it wasn't me. You know what I mean?"

Katie definitely knew what she meant— better than anyone. "Maybe Mrs. Derkman will let you try again," Katie suggested.

"Do you really think so?" Becky asked.

Katie wasn't sure if Mrs. Derkman would give Becky another chance, but it was worth a try. "You're new," Katie told her. "Tell her you got nervous."

"I *was* kind of nervous, waiting for my turn," Becky recalled.

"And maybe you should volunteer to do a different topic," Katie continued. "Then you're doing extra work."

Becky made a face. "Why would I want to do that? I did so much work on my report."

"Yeah, but you already . . ."

Katie was about to say that Becky had already messed up her Cleopatra report, but that wasn't true. Katie had messed it up for her. So instead she said, "Mrs. Derkman likes when kids do extra work. And you want Mrs. Derkman to like you. It's horrible when she's mad at you. Just ask George. She's always angry with him."

"I guess," Becky said thoughtfully. "What topic should I pick?"

"I don't know. Something you're interested in." She stopped for a minute. "You weren't really all that into Cleopatra, were you?"

Becky looked down at the tile floor. "No."

"Then why did you pick that topic?" Katie asked her.

Becky frowned. "I guess Suzanne made it sound so interesting. She makes everything sound interesting."

Katie nodded. "I know what you mean."

"I thought if Suzanne and I had something in common, we'd be friends. And if Suzanne became my friend, then everyone would be my friend," Becky explained.

"Well, a lot of people do like Suzanne," Katie agreed. "But you don't have to be just like her to make friends. Just be yourself."

"But everyone here is so different than the

kids at my old school. Y'all have been friends forever."

Katie shook her head. "Not all of us. George was new at the beginning of the year. He has lots of friends now. You will, too. It just takes time." She smiled. "I'm your friend, so you've got one pal already."

Becky smiled. "Okay, pal," she said sweetly. "Can you help me come up with a report topic?

"Sure! What do you like to do?" said Katie.

Becky thought about that for a minute. "Well, back in Atlanta I took gymnastics. I was getting pretty good at the balance beam and floor exercises."

"So ask Mrs. Derkman if you can do a report on gymnastics," Katie suggested. Then she frowned and touched her nose. It was still sore where George had crashed into her. "Just don't do a cartwheel into my face, okay?"

Becky giggled and stuck out her hand. "It's a deal."

Chapter 10

"Coco Chanel was known for her simple dresses and suits," Suzanne told the class Thursday morning. "She also created costume jewelry and quilted handbags."

"P.U. What's that smell?" George held his nose and looked all around the room. "I think it's coming from *you*, Suzanne."

Suzanne rolled her eyes. "That's perfume," she told George. "Coco Chanel created all sorts of perfumes. Her most famous is called Chanel Number Five."

"She should have called it *Dog Poo* Number Five," George said. "It smells terrible."

"George!" Mrs. Derkman scolded. "We do

not say 'dog poo' in school."

"Oh, I'm not wearing Chanel perfume," Suzanne said. "I made my perfume myself."

"How did you do that?" Mandy asked.

"I used a perfume-making kit," Suzanne explained. "It's a mixture of bubble gum, grape, and rosebud scents. I call it Suzanne Number One."

Then Suzanne showed the class pictures of clothes that Coco Chanel had designed. The girls seemed interested. The boys were bored.

"Lots of designers copied Coco Chanel's work," Suzanne said, as she finished her report. "Everyone wanted to look like her and dress like her. That's why *I* can relate to her."

Mrs. Derkman stood up and smiled at Suzanne. "I knew this would be a good topic for you to research. Thank you for your report." The teacher turned to Becky. "Are you ready?" she asked her.

Becky stood nervously and straightened the sleeves on her blue and silver gymnastics leotard. She looked at Katie.

Katie smiled and gave her a thumbs-up sign.

Becky gave her a thumbs-up back, then. . .

Whoosh! Becky flipped in midair and landed on her hands! She walked upside down to the front of the room.

Whoosh! Becky flipped over again. This time, she landed on her feet.

"My report is about gymnastics," Becky told them. "People have been doing gymnastics for more than two thousand years. But it's only been a competitive sport for about one hundred years."

Becky gave a long speech about about the history of gymnastics. She didn't use any note

cards. She knew it all by heart.

Then Becky demonstrated some of the moves she had learned in her gymnastics classes. She did a back flip, a cartwheel, and a handspring. She ended her routine with a perfect split.

"Awesome!" Jeremy exclaimed.

"I wish I could do that!" George said.

"Can you teach me to do a cartwheel?" Zoe asked. "I always flop over to the side."

Suddenly, everyone was talking at once. They all wanted Becky to teach them how to do gymnastics.

Katie looked at Suzanne. She was playing with her beaded necklace, trying to act as though she didn't like Becky's report. But Katie knew better. It would be impossible not to have found Becky's speech interesting.

"Okay class, settle down," Mrs. Derkman said. "I don't want anyone trying any of Becky's tricks out on the playground. You should only learn gymnastics from a real

gymnastics teacher."

"That's right," Becky said. "My mom found a gymnastics school here in Cherrydale. Maybe some of y'all can take classes there, too."

"Do they have a trampoline?" Miriam said.

"Sure," Becky said.

"How about a vaulting horse?" asked Jeremy.

"Of course."

Becky told the other kids what gymnastics school was like. She didn't seem like a new kid any more. She was one of them now.

There was no reason for Becky to be a copy-cat ever again.

Chapter 11

"This one is called a round-off," Becky said, as she leaped up, flipped, and twisted her body in midair.

"All right, Becky!" Jeremy shouted.

Becky smiled brightly and winked at him. Jeremy blushed.

It was recess. Usually the kids in class 3A would be all over the playground. But today they were all gathered on the grass, watching Becky do her gymnastics. Every time she bent her body or flipped over, they cheered.

Suzanne was the only one in the class not watching Becky. She was sitting all by herself on a bench.

Katie looked over and studied her best friend's face. She looked sad and kind of lonely.

It was weird to see Suzanne like that. Usually Suzanne looked angry, happy, or proud of herself. She never looked sad. And she was *never* alone on the playground. Katie figured the look on Suzanne's face meant trouble for Becky.

And then the strangest thing happened. Becky turned away from the sea of kids surrounding her. She walked over to Suzanne.

"Hi," Becky said shyly.

"What do *you* want?" Suzanne asked.

Becky grinned. "I just wanted to tell you that I thought your report was the best in the whole class. I'd never heard of Coco Chanel before, but now I think she's just the coolest!"

Suzanne smiled . . . a little. "She was pretty cool," she admitted.

"You know what I was thinking?" Becky asked. "You're kind of like the Coco Chanel of our class. You set the fashion trends."

Suzanne's smile broadened. "I was thinking the same thing." She studied Becky's glittery yellow-and-orange shirt. "Some black beads would look really nice with that," she said.

"You think so?" Becky asked her.

Suzanne nodded. "Coco Chanel wore beads with everything!"

"I don't know where to get beads in Cherrydale," Becky admitted. "I wore my mother's red beads the other day."

"There's a great bead shop at the mall. It's near Katie's mom's bookstore," Suzanne said.

Katie's mom worked part time at the Book Nook bookstore in the Cherrydale Mall.

"Maybe you and I could go and look at beads . . . together," Becky suggested shyly.

"Katie and I are going to the mall Saturday morning. We're going to hand out flyers for her mom's store. You could tag along . . . I guess," Suzanne told her.

Becky shook her head. "I have gymnastics

on Saturday mornings."

"Okay." Suzanne began to walk away.

"But I could meet you later, after my class," Becky said quickly.

"We'll be there until three o'clock," Suzanne told her. "If you come earlier, maybe the three of us could get a slice of pizza at Louie's."

"Is that in the mall, too?"

Suzanne nodded.

"Is it good pizza?" Becky asked.

"The best!" Suzanne said. "Boy, you've got a lot to learn about Cherrydale, Becky."

"I'll see you Saturday," Becky assured her. Then she turned and walked back toward the kids on the grass.

Katie made her way across the playground to Suzanne. "What was that all about?"

"Nothing," Suzanne shrugged. "I just told Becky to meet us at the mall on Saturday. That's all. No biggie."

Katie looked surprised. "So you're friends?" she asked.

Suzanne shrugged. "I don't know about friends . . ." she began. "She's okay, I guess."

"Yeah, Becky's pretty okay," Katie agreed.

"You know, I was thinking," Suzanne continued, "I like dressing like Coco Chanel because she was so cool, smart, and creative. Maybe that's the reason Becky has been acting the way she has. She wants to be like me. Who wouldn't?"

Katie choked back a laugh. Sometimes Suzanne could be so full of herself.

"Besides, Becky's new here," Suzanne continued. "She needs someone with my experience—and flair for fashion—to show her around."

That made Katie angry. She'd been showing Becky around all week. And she'd done a good job of making her feel at home. Katie was about to tell Suzanne just that, when she suddenly felt a cold breeze blowing all around her.

Oh, no! Was the magic wind back? Would it blow with Suzanne standing right there?

"Katie, what's the matter with you?"
Suzanne asked. "You look look like you just
saw a ghost." Suzanne held her palm up in the
air. "I think I just felt a raindrop. And listen
to that wind. I think we're going to have a
storm."

Katie breathed a sigh of relief. Suzanne
could hear the wind, too. This was just a
regular storm—the kind everybody could feel.

"I hate rain!" Suzanne moaned.

"The flowers need it. And so do the trees," Katie told her.

Suzanne smiled. "That's why you're my best friend," she said.

"Huh?"

"You're always thinking about someone else," Suzanne explained. "Like the trees. Or Becky. You really wanted to help her."

Katie gulped. *Help her?* Katie had almost ruined everything for her.

But, of course, Suzanne didn't know anything about that.

"I just told her to do a report on something *she* found interesting," Katie said quickly.

Suzanne nodded. "And that report helped her make friends. You knew what she needed. I swear, Katie, sometimes it's like you can get right inside other people's brains."

Katie started to laugh. Inside people's brains? Suzanne didn't know the half of it!

Chapter 12

Did you ever wonder how we know so much about the lives of people in ancient Egypt? Becky found the answer to that question while she was researching Cleopatra. (Of course Suzanne already knew the answer, but that's another story!)

It turns out the ancient Egyptians had a written language. But they didn't use letters in their alphabet. They used pictures. Each picture stood for a sound.

The ancient Egyptians used their picture language to write stories about their lives on the walls of their buildings and pyramids.

At the library, Becky found a chart that

shows the Egyptian alphabet. Now she, Katie, and Suzanne can send notes to each other in ancient Egyptian.

That's going to make Mrs. Derkman really mad. After all, she doesn't have a copy of this chart.

But you do!

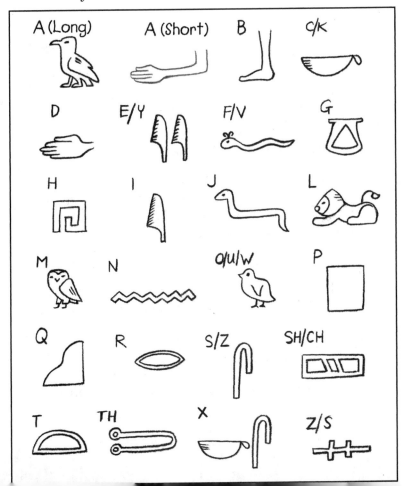